a contagious mind

By: Tyler Vo

Writing saved my life;
> now I can only hope mine impacts yours.

Copyright © 2018 by Tyler Vo
All rights reserved. This book or any portion thereof may not be reproduced or used in any manner whatsoever without the express written permission of the publisher except for the use of brief quotations in a book review.

ISBN 978-1-7907-3820-5

(Phase One: Elementary School)

Rocks

We used to play with rocks.
We liked the way they crumbled like sand.
We liked how soft they were.
Sure. Mommy bought us lots of toys but the rocks were our favorite-
Daddy always left them around when he came home:
The rocks were our little secret.
They were different from the rocks at the park and on the ground.
They looked cleaner. They were even shiny sometimes!
Mommy caught Danny playing with rocks one time;
She yelled at Daddy before she took the rocks away from Danny.
We never let her catch us again.

Our oldest brother Jerrold never played with us though.
J only came down to play when there were no rocks around.
He would teach us how to play sports and board games.
NO ROCKS He said. That was his only rule.
It always made us sad that he didn't want to play with us
But we wanted to be just like J so we followed his rules.

One time I brought some rocks to school to play with-
I wanted to show my friends.
They never had as nice of toys as me;
I always brought new toys for them to play with.
This time, I wanted to show them my favorite:
The rocks.

Why are they white? They asked.
They're special rocks. My Daddy brings them home.
My friends were very excited.
Now they could come over and play with us!

On the bus home, I looked and saw Jerrold in the back.
He looked mad.

When we got off I waited for him outside
What the do you think you're doing Dre? Are you stupid?
I didn't say anything.
I started crying. I didn't know why J was yelling at me.
He grabbed me by the shirt and dragged me away from all the other kids:

What's on your pants Dre?
I looked down and saw white dust on my trousers.
My rocks probably just got crushed a little. I can clean them! Mom won't notice!
J stared at me. Still angry.
You brought the rocks… to school? Give them to me.
I started crying again.
I reached into my pocket and gave J the crushed up rocks.
Fuck. You better clean your pants off before we get in the house.
I continued to sob while I brushed off my pants.
I knew J didn't like the rocks but why was he yelling at me?
We walked home in silence.
I could hear J cursing under his breath next to me.
He turned to look at me.
You're one stupid kid, you know that Dre? Stupid.

Stupid. Stupid. Stupid.
The word rang in my head all afternoon after I came home.
I cried myself to sleep before waking up for dinner.
Why was Jerrold being so mean to me?
I thought he liked me most!
Stupid.
Stupid Dre. I told myself.
And why did he take away my rocks? Why was J so mad?
The thought of making J mad made me sad again.
I lost my rocks and J called me stupid.
That was a sad day.

Family

My Mommy is the prettiest woman in the world.
She makes the world a happy place when she smiles.
She buys me lots of toys and cooks me yummy food.
I love her a lot.
She's the bestest mommy!
Even when she yells at us.
She can get scary but I know it's because she loves us too!
Her and Daddy fight a lot.
Her and Daddy also laugh and smile together a lot.
I guess that's what parents do.

My Daddy is the smartest man in the world.
He works all the time and buys us cool things around the house
Like the TV's and the couches and the beds and the phones.
He even drives a spaceship!
For Christmas last year he got Mommy a racecar so they could drive together.
All their cars are so cool.
My friends get jealous when Mommy drops us off at school.
Daddy says he works so much so that mommy doesn't have to.
I think Daddy is a superhero. He protects us and keeps us happy and safe.
He talks on his phone a lot.
He always leaves dinner early to talk on the phone.
He sometimes doesn't come home from work.
He's a very busy man.

My brother Jerrold is the best big brother in the world.
He takes care of me and Danny.
He helps me and Danny with homework.
He teaches us how to play games and sports.
He does our chores for us sometimes without telling anyone.
He gets really mad at us when we play with rocks though.
I think Jerrold gets in fights at school. He comes home with bruises and scratches.
He tells me not to tell Mommy.

I keep all of J's secrets because he would kill me if I told anyone!
I hope Jerrold doesn't get bullied.
That makes me sad.
I love Jerrold. I want to be just like him when I grow up!

My twin brother Danny is just like me.
We were born at the same time and we do everything together!
He likes to play with rocks with me.
We hide them from J and Mommy.
Danny is better than me at sports
But I beat him at all the board games.
Jerrold says it's because Danny is stronger
And I'm smarter.
But J called me stupid. I always remember that.
Danny and I share a room and we sometimes stay up past bedtime to play
Sometimes our teachers get us mixed up.
I heard Mommy say we're identical. That means we look alike.
Danny and I can never be separated. We'll be together forever!

Secrets

On my 9th birthday Jerrold told me that he had a big birthday present for me.
He said I wouldn't like it.
I loved my birthday.
But this time I just wanted to know what Jerrold got me!
I waited all day and every time I saw him I thought he would give me his gift.
After dinner, I still hadn't gotten his gift.
I had a pile of presents in the living room.
I hadn't opened any of them. I was waiting for J.

Why don't you open your presents sweetheart? Danny already did. My mom asked.
I'm waiting for J! He says he has a gift for me
Mommy smiled at me. She walked back upstairs.
While I was sitting and waiting I decided to look at some of the presents.

I noticed Daddy left a present by the fireplace.
It was big. Almost bigger than me.
I smiled. I got excited.
I sat back down and waited some more.
J never came down with his gift.
I guess I'll open these tomorrow. I thought to myself.
I was too sad to open presents. My birthday was ruined.

I couldn't sleep that night.
I closed my eyes. I counted sheep. Nothing!
Then my door opened slowly.
Jerrold!
I sat up in bed.
Are you giving me my present now? I asked excitedly.
Yes. But I told you you're not gonna like it, little bro.
My smile turned into a frown. I didn't get it.
Why not? Why would you give me something I don't like?
J looked at me very seriously.
Come sit down on the floor with me, Dre.
I hopped out of bed and sat down with him.
He checked to see if Mommy was asleep. He closed the door.
Daddy didn't come home that day.

Danny. Get down here, too. I know you're listening.
Danny sat up in bed and jumped off and ran over to us.
He sat down excitedly.
Do I get a big gift too? Danny asked J.
Yes. Both of you are getting a gift. The same one.
Danny and I looked at each other. We were confused.
I didn't want the same gift as Danny.

Look. I never wanted to do this. But I have to. You guys are my baby brothers. And you need to know. I figured I'd tell you guys now before you get older and find out some other way. I just want you guys to know that I love both of you. Very much. This stays between us three. Got it? You guys have to promise me you won't tell anyone. Especially your friends.

Now I was very confused.
Me and Danny nodded.

I don't know if you guys are mature enough to handle this, but you're gonna have to learn to grow up starting now because I was your guys' age when I found out-

Found out what? I interrupted.

Shut up and let me finish, Dre. 5 years ago, when I was 9, I found out the truth, Dre. I found out what Dad does and why Mom doesn't let you guys play with the rocks. Why I don't play with the rocks anymore. Dad... he's a dope dealer. He sells drugs to some really rich, messed up people. Dad's a rich, powerful, scary man. He loves us. But he's involved with a lot of dark, messed up things. I can't explain them to you right now but you'll learn. It's fucked up. All of it. The money. The clothes. The TV's. The games. The cars. Everything. That's how he buys all that stuff for us.

 God, I hated seeing you guys get so attached to those damn rocks. Ever since you guys were just babies you played with the rocks. They got all over your hands, your faces and I would have to wash them off before Mom saw. Dad? He doesn't give a shit. He has so much money and power. That's all he really gives a shit about. But Jesus Christ, guys. They're fucking CRACK ROCKS. You guys are playing with fucking crack rocks. I wanted to keep you away from them but you kept on playing with them and I couldn't tell you.. I just couldn't..

Danny and I sat there staring at J.
We didn't notice he was crying until he stopped talking.
I started crying. Danny started crying.
I felt an arm pull me and Danny in.

Until now. I couldn't tell you guys until now. But you needed to know. It's fucked up. I'm sorry. I wish I could have kept this all a secret from you two.

Stay away from the rocks, okay? Stay away from Dad, stay away from his business, stay away from everything he puts his hands on. Dad's not a bad guy. He just does bad things. But that's how we get to live how we live. Understand? Just stay away from the rocks. Please...

Jerrold was sobbing now.
I had never seen J cry. Until now.
I started crying again. Danny just sat there.

We sat on the ground for a few more hours.
Danny fell asleep. J picked him up and brought him to bed.
He came back and sat down with me.
I was not sleeping that night.

I'm sorry, Dre. I'm sorry. I love you guys. I need you guys to be smart. I need you guys to grow up. I need you guys to help me help Mom. I need you guys to be MEN. Can you do that?

I looked up at my brother.
I had so many questions. But I was tired.
I wanted to sleep. My birthday was ruined.

After Jerrold left, I climbed into bed and tried to sleep.
I closed my eyes.
I need you guys to be MEN.
I couldn't sleep.
I need you guys to be MEN.
How could we be men? We were only 9 years old!
I need you guys to be MEN.
I couldn't sleep.
My birthday was ruined.

(Phase 2: Middle School)

Dre

Andre Milton Washington
7th Grade.
13 years old.
Black. Light Skinned.
2 Brothers:
Daniel Matthew Washington. Jerrold Marcus Washington.
2 Parents:
Makami "Mac" Washington. Rebecca Amelia Olsen.
Born and raised in Los Angeles, California.
Hobbies include: hanging out with friends, playing sports, traveling.
Favorite subject in school: English.
Favorite candy: M&M's.
Wants to be an astronaut when he grows up.
Goal for this year: grow four inches.
Andre Milton Washington

(Phase 3: Adulthood)

Santa "Mac"

I knew the kids at school were jealous.
I could physically feel their encroaching envy with every passing glance.
When I was younger, innocence spared me the everyday ritual of pretending to ignore
All the beady eyes and hushed whispers constantly surrounding me
As I walked down the hallway minding my own business.

I couldn't help it.
Momma always bought me the nicest shirts and the nicest shoes.
I was grateful. Don't get it twisted.
But it was middle school:
The same kids that reveled in awe were the ones that schemed in darkness about vandalism and petty theft.
I knew. I was aware.

It was never my intention to flaunt my family's wealth directly in the faces of my peers as a King would to belittle his subjects
But people talk. And kids love to listen.

Rich boy.
Prep.
Bitch.
Spoiled.
Stuck up.
Conceited.
Arrogant.
Pussy.
Uncle Tom.

My response was always absent much like many of their fathers.
Not because naught I had to say, but because I had no interest in entertaining their existence.
Much like many of their fathers.

Christmas was always my favorite holiday.
Although Momma and Pops always levied a steady stream of gifts to us regularly, they kept us on our toes with plenty of surprises during the holiday season.
This year, however, I was remiss about the festivities.
The child in me remained overjoyed with tearing open wrapping paper and marveling at the wonderful pile of presents with my two brothers.
But my heart drifted outside the warm, cozy bubble in that living room that night.

My mind wandered into the near future:
I knew that my classmates, while enjoying their own Christmas, were waiting to see what new gear I would come to school with.
Salivating at the fresh opportunity to scuff and stain my privilege with their classless derogation and insults.
I took a pass on the eggnog in exchange for feigned excitement blended with genuine, but guilty appreciation.

The night before I went back to school I woke up from a flustered, trainwreck performance of attempted sleep early in the morning before anybody else in the house.
I found myself sprinting down the street in my pajamas towards the park with my duffel bag in hand, panting heavily.
I walked up slowly to the dumpster.

My walk back home as the sun began to rise felt much lighter.

Vacuum

Sometimes I wish I was in space floating by myself
No one around me
Just a vacuum suffocating my cries for help.
A sunken place but with a way to Get Out.
A place so densely vast its infinity begins to compress me.

My thoughts would travel out boundlessly,
A series of transverse waves gliding aimlessly
Searching for metaphysical destinations always just slightly out of reach.

The obstructions of everyday life take many shapes and forms:
Human interaction,
Impeding and interrupting the natural flow of self-
Walls,
An enigmatic symbol of protection and entrapment living in simultaneity-
Emotions,
Fleeting yet abhorrently destructive and alluring-
All of which, amongst many more, boast a propensity to derail us from our intrinsic complacency and innateness.

In this vacuum I define the parameters of my existence:
A wormhole branching together the sounds of my thoughts and the silence of my echoing voice;
A tear in the seams of space just big enough to fit me into its infinite pocket;
It's comforting being able to place myself in the center of my orbit;

In this vacuum I've never mattered more
And in this vacuum I've never felt so small

Battle Scars

I didn't hear the footsteps running behind me.
My headphones blocked out the voices calling my name.
My eyes couldn't see the target painted across my back.

They caught me right before I could turn the corner onto my street.

I felt a hand grab my shoulder and spin me around.
My eyes widened as I caught sight of a fist inches away from my face.
Futilely and fruitlessly I raised my arms in defense
As the fist connected with my left eye,
Knocking me down on the pavement in a blundering fall.
Before I could open my eyes again, two quick blows struck either side of my ribcage
Sending a flurry of nociceptors up to my brain as I could hear my right side give way to a small crack.

Fuck you, you little spoiled bitch!

Yeah, where's your brother to save you?

You ain't shit. You're just a weak, pathetic loser.

The taunts barely seeped through my ringing and bloodied ears.
I continued to brace for impact as a barrage of swift punches to my face
and stomach broke momentarily only for a couple agonizing kicks
That persisted in both breaking my body as well as my consciousness.

I lay on the cold cement waiting for the next grueling series of attacks but was met with more taunting and laughing.

Yo take his shoes! They're expensive.

I got his headphones!

Numb and absolutely shattered, I opened my eyes slowly to see three boys removing the sneakers off my feet and ripping the headphones out of my phone and off my neck.

The same blood that filled my throat covered my face
As I coughed up the crimson, sanguine fluid.
Tears streamed down my face.
I lay motionless on the ground.
Helpless. Weak. Pathetic.

My mind lay awake amidst the brutalization and devastation that left my body mangled;
I screamed internally while my mouth began to sew itself shut.
Even in my deadened state I could feel my eyes begin to roll backwards as I struggled to breathe.
My corpse ushered one last comforting shiver
Before I succumbed to the insidious chill inhabiting every fiber of my being.

Hospital Bed

Stiff pillows
Forced reclination
Heavily constrained mobility
Slipping consciousness
Lack of appetite
Unfamiliar faces

Awake
Asleep
Awake
Pass out

Every morning starts with a startled awakening
Incognizant of how the last episode ended.
Like falling asleep during a movie
And never knowing where you left off the night before.

My mind wanders when my eyes muster the strength to open
Aimlessly, but not tirelessly.
A quick stroll through the synapses is exhausting.
But what else is there to do when one is merely an inanimate shell?

Momma always came to visit me with Danny.
Sometimes they would sleep next to me.
Pops came by once I think.
I never saw Jerrold.

Whenever someone walks in the room, I hear them before I see them;
My eyes open slowly and take an eternity to focus on the blurry face peering down on me.
I hope to see J standing there smiling.
I wonder where J is.

I stayed in the hospital for 3 weeks.
I never physically felt any better during that time.
The dullness of the room complemented the numbness in my body
Like how the whistle of a bird brings out the crisp air of an early morning.

The last night I was in the hospital I was in exceptional pain:
It was one of those nights where it was too much to even open my eyes.
I lay there awake on that stiff hospital bed with my eyes closed
Pondering what the next 24 hours would bring.

I heard someone come into the room.
I kept my eyes closed and focused on trying to fall asleep.
The nurse made no noise as her feet shuffled around on the floor.
Soon I was alone in the rigid silence again.

I awoke to a shadowy overcast morning
With the dim beams of lights streaming onto my face.
My eyes peered open tediously
To a sight that made my heart tremble:

On the cart next to my bed were my sneakers and headphones from the day I got jumped.
I noticed the scuffs on the sneakers were scrubbed off. Just like new.
I began sobbing uncontrollably as pure, unadulterated joy sewed together my cracked body.
It was Jerrold.

Cords

He hasn't spoken a word in weeks! You have to talk to your son, Mac.

He'll snap out of it eventually. Kid just got his ass kicked. I wouldn't say nothing to nobody either.

My voice died the day I couldn't.
When my ribs fractured and my body went numb, the animation in my cries died as my tears dried around my battered eyes.
When I didn't come home that night, my brother found my remains lying on the curb,
The taunts and cowardice of my assailants branded on me
Their inarticulate and barbaric designs found in every bruise and fracture.
They were able to drag me to a hospital before the palpitations reached their expiration
But my voice was nowhere to be found.

To this day, they could send a search team to the farthest realms of hell and back and they'd come back with nothing.
The words in my mouth were taken from me and beaten to submission with excessive force.
If I had known Silence would co-sign my mind I would have kept my mouth shut
And savor the cries I wasted so desperately for no one to hear.

My voice died so I didn't have to
Its sacrifice the reason why I wake up every day:
Silent with no words but plenty to say.

Dog Days

It's the kind of heat that makes you feel relaxed and serene, not on edge
A warm glow that sweeps over every inch of your body
Quite sharp and synchronously at first, but then gently as you continue to step out into the sunlight.
The raw power of the sun invigorates every fiber from within you,
The sensation of constrained freedom makes your soul salivate with thirst.
People smile more during this time of year:
At least that's what it feels like.

As you stroll out onto the shiny, sizzling pavement, a rough blend of aridity and charcoal rushes through your nostrils and squeezes every which alveolus in your lungs.
Your hoarse cough emanates discomfort, but you enjoy the smell.
Your neighbors are barbecuing.
Your body succumbs to the aroma, your neck turning sharply towards the smoke.
You lock eyes and smiles with a friendly face and exchange hand waves.
Turning away, you notice how infectious that beam of joy radiating from a smile truly is.
No matter how hard you try, you can't wipe the delight off your face.

Smiling. Must be something about this time of year.

You hop into your car and immediately the suffocating claustrophobia of densely packed heat rushes towards you,
Causing you to perspire just a bit while you start the engine and crank up the A/C.
You quickly roll the windows down, allowing the internal heat to escape as you drive off down the street.

The blistering sun continues to beat down on the mortal souls vulnerable to its ultraviolet casting
But you don't feel a thing.
The magnificent breeze cools you off like an icy wave of refreshment while you speed down the highway.

With nothing but unimpeded road staring you down, you close your eyes for just a brief moment:

Oh what a feeling.
Unperturbed by whimsical trivialities, you allow yourself to soak in the dazzling array of sunlight above one last time before opening your eyes.
A wide smile makes it away across your face.

Must be something about this time of year.

Residence

I came home from the hospital 3 days ago but home didn't feel like home:
My bed smelled like it had been rented out to the highest bidder at a misery auction.
My clothes fit as if they had been tailored for someone with broad shoulders, slim torso, and a will to live.
Who plucked me out of that dismal hospital bed and placed me in this cage built for feigned happiness and existential purpose?

My room is a cloud on which I rest upon
Barely moving as to prevent the very real possibility of falling off and crashing to my death
Keenly observing all that goes on around me:
Parents arguing
Parents watching and prodding me at my every change in countenance, looking for answers to quell their guilt
J popping in and out of the house
Danny asking me to play.

Growing Up Different

The bullets didn't wait for an answer
They just rang.
The fireworks didn't start until after nightfall
But there was nothing to celebrate.
We never saw them coming.
By the time we heard the crack of the hammer
The barks of strays had already zipped by our heads.

GET DOWN

I heard my father yell from the living room.

I fell to the ground and covered my head as glass rained down on me
I could hear the yells and gunfire encroaching slowly towards the house

Closer and closer.
Louder and louder.

I began crawling to the living room towards my father's voice.
I thought about where Danny was
Where my mom was
Where J was

When I got to the living room, the gunfire stopped.
I saw Dad rifling through the drawers in the corner of the room;
He turned around, a pistol in each hand, shoving what looked like a shotgun towards me.

Pick that up, son. I'm gonna need you to throw that to me when I ask you to. Okay? You got that, kid?

I stared at him blankly.
I scurried over to my dad, dragging the shotgun along with me.

They kicked down the front door
Opening our house to bullet spray and yelling threats.

Where you at motherfucker?

Get out here. Show your face, bitch!

I sat down crying next to my father around the corner, only feet away from the front door.
There was no way we were getting out of here alive.

The first man who stepped inside our house was welcomed with two bullets to the chest.
His body dropped to the floor just as quickly as it entered with a loud thud.
I opened my eyes to see my dad peering out with his gun aimed at the door.
A flurry of steps flooded in complemented by equally sporadic gunfire.
Once again, Dad turned to his left and fired off a couple rounds.

Another body fell to the floor.

This time my dad turned around in a hurry as a myriad of bullets came flying in our direction.

Keep your head down! I'm gonna need that shotgun now, Dre.

I handed my dad the shotgun and he threw one of the pistols back at me.

My gaze traveled down to the pistol sitting in my lap;
Its clean, shiny barrel reflected a stern look back at me.
My hands shaking uncontrollably, I picked up the gun.
I closed my eyes briefly and fainted as the trigger manifested itself, the grip searing into the palm of my hand.

NULL

What can we settle for when we're insatiably unsatisfied?
Humans will spit out the very rain they yearn for
Always expecting to see more.
Knowing there'd be more.
There's an insidious danger to wielding the double-edged sword of ambition we push with such pride
The farther we carry it, the heavier it drags us down,
Breaking our backs and cutting our hands as we struggle to keep our feet moving
The scars on our backs tell the tales of the places we've been
The roads we've crossed
The souls we've intertwined and claimed
The hearts we've seen and touched
The trails and marks we've left behind.
But we only feel the pain and ache wound in every stitch and fiber of our scars.
We can't see the stories we've created
We don't take the time out to look around at what's in front of us while we're there
Our mind baffles itself grinding its dusty, foreign gears trying to pull up the memories
Our eyes fixate themselves on the future.
Tunnel vision blinds us from our own lives

We can never stop wanting.
Our need is our want.
We don't want the sun, we want the white light;
Its purity and perfection captivates us
But why stop there?

We want the whole damn spectrum.

We need to have everything at once
And that,
That is what leaves us with

Well, I want something.

Fine.

Our Hollow Home

Jerrold lost his way sometime last May
Consumed with money and greener fields, the game he couldn't leave it
The apple falls closer to the tree than they say
If you had told me J's shooters came for my dad I wouldn't believe it
Nothing about it makes sense to me.

Mom refused to believe J tried to murder Dad
But I guess I finished his job for him.
I wasn't surprised when J disappeared the day Dad died
The day I killed my own father.
He was trying to build his empire this whole time-
Now he had it.

I thought I would see him on the corner or around the city
But I only saw some of his old friends driving around in their new cars
Flashing their jewelry and guns.
They'd stare me down with the barrel of their pistols
And laugh as they sped off.
I couldn't decide if I felt oddly safe or rightfully terrified

I think often about how J would make sure I kept up with school
And that I had a plan for college and beyond.
He talked fantastically about becoming a doctor and saving lives
And now he sends people to the Emergency Room as a pitstop to hell.
I contemplated packing up and leaving as well.
But Mom didn't have the energy to go.
So now we exist in the darkness of our home, or rather its shell,
Somewhere between oblivion and hell.

This Dance

Nervousness
Not quite anxiety but more serene
The kind that resembles butterflies
And heavy excitation.

We do this every time we meet.

Our eyes switch back and forth
Between the ground,
The wall,
Each other,
The lights.

Like a camera held with shaky hands
We're too afraid to blink
Or keep our gaze fixed for too long
Preoccupied with capturing just the right moment.
A still frame through restless lens
The world hustles busily in the background:
A timelapse of our apprehensive emotions.

Something beckons me towards you
But the invisible hand guiding me loses sight of its destination.
Our feet are itching to move
But our hearts beat with different rhythms.

The song dwindles down to a subtle end.
I glance back down at the ground nervously;
Maybe one day we'll finish what we started

Eternity

My heart aches for a new day even before this one's gone
The thought of new horizons makes me want to fast forward from dusk to dawn
My fingers itch when the night starts to call-
Being able to capture the wealth of tomorrow before squandering today
Magnifies my insatiable appetite for the invigorating nutrients
Found in life's every molecule and fiber.

People like to say they're going soul searching.
As if to say they're embarking on the proverbial journey of self-revelation
That only adjourns upon reaching some grandiose self-fulfilling prophecy.
It ends when they find the sole thing that defines their humanity.
I say sole as in the sole soul that one owns:
A soul that has wandered as far as the soles under one's own feet.

My lust lies in the boundless youth exhibited by the atomic clock responsible for the planets' orbits;
The metaphysical shrewdness of electron waves whose frequencies turn the gears of space-time
Compels me to relentlessly seek the interminable perpetuation locked within the tantalizing realm of infinity.

While others remain preoccupied with retrieving what was already once theirs,
My search for self-realization begins with reaching out to years of passing light
With an open-palmed, boundlessly optimistic outstretched hand-
Grasping at figments of blinking stars breeding eternal wisdom,
Consumed with the promise of immortality.

Jack Frost

I awoke to a crisp breeze drifting through the open window;
Sharp as a knife, slicing through the dense smog
That chokes the Angels of the city every hour of the day.
The smell of the air was so pungent and sweet,
Yet foreign enough to demand my full attention as I skipped most of my morning routine to walk outside.
I noticed it was oddly bright out, albeit the sky was coated with an opaque mass of clouds.
The cold wind chilled me down to my bones.
Not biting, but gently poking through my skin and gripping onto my nerves firmly.
My lungs became quickly enamored with the fresh, clean air.
I must have stood there motionless for 15 minutes before
I heard the engine of a car drive down the street,
Breaking my tantalizingly tranquil trance;
The all too familiar smell of smoke and exhaust trespassing through my nose.
I scanned around to see if anybody else had noticed our new Neighbor this morning.
My street was completely empty without a single breath of life escaping the cozy confines of December homes.
I swear the wind intensified while I was staring blankly at the world
So I began to walk back towards the front door, shivering just slightly.
There was an increasingly overt moisture rising in the air.
I could feel the wetness softly blanketing my face as I hurried back into my house.
I opened the window wider to welcome in the draft and then crawled back into bed to catch some more sleep before my alarm went off.

When I woke up two hours later, my eyes were met with a blinding white glare coming from outside.
The sun must have come out!
I noticed the floor was wet but thought nothing of it as I walked to the kitchen.

And that's when I looked outside and saw glittering balls of cotton floating slowly down onto the ground.
And that's the day LA welcomed Jack Frost into its neighborhood for the first time in 54 years.

Shadows of a Ghost

The same night Pops died, J ran away.
Disappeared into thin air; only told me he couldn't stay
It would've been his 19th birthday today.
I remember every year I would wait in his room all day
Anxiously testing my patience until he finally peered through the doorway;
I would jump on him and sing him 'Happy Birthday'
While he slowly pulled me off of him in shy dismay.
Shaking his head he would say thanks and ask me what game I wanted to play.
Every year, same thing
But I guess you can never get used to things staying the same way
When everything you've ever known is birthed from disarray.

Danny started having fits and Momma was never around.
I tried finding a job, one where I needn't talk
And sometimes I'd wake up to Momma crying on the ground;
The quiver in her voice made the floors creak, made it hard to walk
Without tearing up, trying not to make a sound.
Watching her tremble with the eternal aftershock
Of seeing her husband's blood paint the walls of her sanctuary
Brought me to my knees as I struggled to grasp
The weight of pain she carries when she wakes.

I always wanted to be like Jerrold
But I would never leave Momma behind.
He slipped into the night like a ghost,
Leaving his family in the dark
Like an estranged deadbeat abandons his children.
During the day, the invisible shadows of dead men walking
Cast looming clouds of fear and unknown over our cemetery;
During the day, the shadows made it night.
In the night, the shadows haunted my every step
As the ghosts rose out of their graves to flirt with the demons in my head.
The road before me had abruptly forked into two dim paths;

I toiled with and tormented myself endlessly, not wanting to set foot on either
But refusing to fall off the edge.
I always wanted to be like Jerrold
But I never imagined I'd be chasing the footsteps of a ghost.

Career Day

Office job attire:
Shoes, check
Black socks, check
White shirt buttoned all the way to the top, check
It's Monday so the red tie today, check
Tie clip? Optional, so no check
Belt, check
Watch? We'll leave the Rolex at home today, it's only the first day
Wallet, phone, keys, check

Briefcase:
Pens, check
Legal pad, check
Phone charger, check
Mints, (gotta have those) check
Folder, check
Granola bar, check
Extra resumés and tax forms, check
Laptop? Relax. It's just your first day; leave it behind

Alright let's head out. Don't wanna be late on the first day.

---

hummingbird

my mind wanders when im not with you.
like a bird flying south for the first time
just drifting off over the horizon
with no destination in mind;
i wish i could just follow my heart
but that bat is blind
and i cant trust him anymore.
i know you got demons too, we all do
but mine claw and scratch at my back
with every waking step.
you dont know how hard it is to walk with one eye forward and one over your shoulder.
im a clumsy trip waiting to happen
but i only want to fall for you
and land in the tender palm of your hand.
my body weakens at a glimpse of your eyes
and my thoughts slip when you smile.
you told me when we were kids that we would get married
i wonder if youve forgotten?
or if youll follow through with your promise.
but i dont know if i can wait any longer
for you to bring me out of the darkness to share your spotlight
because wow does it shine bright on you.

ive never felt smaller than when im with you.
my heart flutters 53 beats per second
but my wings havent gotten big enough to take flight with you
as you dive perilessly into lifes canyons
with unparalleled grace and ease.
so i watch on from the nest
waiting restlessly for you to return one day
or for me to gather the courage to jump.
youve always given me the push i needed to face my fears
but you left me on my own
only holding on to the faint whisper of your voice in the wind

trailing back years in the rearview.
i hope you still think of me
because i havent stopped since you left.
im just waiting. waiting for you to come home and fix this broken promise of yours.

CLL

Overcrowding.
Complex canals and pathways filled with microscopic vehicles transporting essential packages of life to your precious organs
Shuddered and blocked by oncoming traffic that nobody saw coming.
As the roads struggle to expand in time to alleviate this influx of trespassing cells,
It feels as though the entire world is collapsing with exhaustion.
Desperate, struggling,
Relinquishing space to foreign invaders;
Time's running out.
B cell lymphocytes overpopulating the nodes, marrow, and streams
Killing off innocent respiratory children every second.
The destruction wages on and on.
You can feel the pain the trees and the earth feels as our highways
Continue to expand and swell,
Encroaching on any remaining sanctuaries.
We've observed this ritual conquest time and time again,
Always hoping it wouldn't happen to us;
It couldn't happen to us.
We were ready. We were prepared.
But it doesn't matter.

Justice

Smoke squeezed out from his dry lips as he stood
Brazen, gazing across the dimly lit street.
A torrential downpour continues to shutter down on the pavement,
Washing away any semblance of consciousness hovering over him.
His arm mechanically raises the barely lit cigarette up to his mouth
He inhales the tar while the smoke slides up through his nostrils
He lets out a tired breath, almost a sigh-

The sirens screeching through the entire city finally enter the scene.
A distraught crowd has formed across the street
Clamoring in awed trauma, frantically looking for the emergency response vehicle
That has kept them waiting for an eternity.

The man observes the scene unfold in front of him without a blink of an eye
The cigarette in his hand has burnt out
As he stands motionless.
His eyes peer slowly from the throng of screaming bystanders
To the paramedics scrambling, shoving their way through.
Water streaks down his face from his soaked hair
But he doesn't notice.
His eye remain fixed on the star of the show.
The main attraction.

The clouds looming over finally see the man lying on the ground as the assembly disperses
And the EMT's get their first glimpse.
Three bullet wounds to the abdomen and one where the eyes meet.
Blood continues to flow down the street, soaking into the soles of every sneaker, boot, and loafer in sight.
Our heroes back away slowly and begin packing up.
Time to abort the rescue mission.

His plane of vision finally breaks as he looks down at his new Patek piece

He wipes off a drop of blood from the face of the watch.
It now glistens in the streetlight.
80,000 and he didn't even spend a dime.
With his other hand he tucks the smoking gun behind his back

For a brief moment his mind wanders to the same picture as every time before.
A boy with his arm wrapped around his younger brother
Both smiling and beaming with pride.
"J+D Summer '99" reads the caption under the polaroid.
His mouth moves as to say something but nothing comes out

Light

You begged and pleaded with me not to sell the house
But what choice did I have?
Working a dead end job because my words refuse to make a sound.
It's not like we needed it anymore now that J's not around.
How did everything get turned so upside down?
I know it broke your heart but I did it anyway
Cuz ain't shit compare to what I've gone through
But I'd still go to hell and back ten times over just to see you light up the world with your smile another day.
Nothing's been the same since pops passed away
But you always kept it together
Even when the darkness decided to settle in and stay.
My silence, I know it frustrated you and kept you awake
But I've been beaten and broken,
Constantly trying to find excuses to live another day.
And the bills weren't getting paid.
Notices were piling up, I couldn't keep being late.
I was stupid and selfish so I hit up J
And got myself a nice gig slinging crack to dope fiends down on Slauson and Broadway.
Your treatments weren't working the doctors were counting down the days;
I engulfed myself in my trade I stopped coming to see you
I avoided coming to grips with the fact that you weren't gonna make it through
So I hustled and trapped to distract myself from the truth
That my mind had become a storm of misery, a suicidal typhoon.
I disappointed you and you weren't conscious half the time to even know it.
I stared down the barrel of a 9 taunting myself to place my fucking brain on a target and blow it
But I made so much money my struggles were barely showing.
I slept less and drank more
Til my mind couldn't fucking think anymore.
I wanted to scream. I wanted to shout.

But the words just couldn't find a way out of my mouth.
I remember when you told me my words were my sword and told me to wield it proud
But I'm a useless mute surrounded by thoughts that won't come out.
The silence in my heart is deafening the darkness it's so loud
I'm ashamed of what I've become I need your guidance here and now.
I miss you so much Momma I don't know what to do.
I wish you could come down to me so I can hold you
And kiss you with these trembling lips that have long lost their use.
I lost my soul the day that I lost you
Because I abandoned you that day in the hospital.
God you made a mistake, it should've been my life for you to take.
I guess that's the price I had to pay
Cuz as every day passes the knife in my heart penetrates deeper
And I'm reminded of the fact that when your breath whimpered and finally started to fade,
I was too busy selling fucking drugs to be by your side to tell you I loved you.
I'm sorry Momma, I hope you can forgive me too.

Sam

Her name was Sage.
Wiser than Solomon was she
The kindness in her heart radiating with every step she took.
Her stoic expression projecting the lessons and struggles of
All the authors, poets, philosophes, scholars and artists
Whose works you'd always find her nose buried in.
She sat with an air of rigid authenticity and smooth deliverance
Her gaze more stern than that of a predatory hawk.
Sage made me think.
Made me ponder my very existence.
Sage made me love pure thought.
And I think about her to this very day.

Her name was Amelie.
A diverse melting pot of ancestry was she
French, Italian, and Filipina
The daughter of working class immigrants,
Amelie wore both the plights and successes of migrant families on her back
Usually in the form of a printed floral pattern
On a beautiful, fragrant sundress
That she loved to twirl so carelessly in.
She absorbed every bit and piece of humanism around her
Blending it together in her colorful soul.
She held on to the most miniscule souvenirs
To add to her boundless collection of memories and experiences.
Amelie instilled in me a yearning appetite to explore different cultures
And the multifaceted wonders of every one.
Amelie taught me to love humanity and its vast diversity
And her welcoming acceptance of others shines through me to this very day.

Her name was Marilyn.
Graceful as an angel was she
Beautiful as the setting sun and as breathtaking as the rising one.

Her skin was soft like the fuzzy inside of a sweater.
Her lips deceptively tender but never hesitating to
Spit daggers that split poor admirers' hearts open.
She had a walk that could give a nihilist purpose
A walk so cold it froze men in their steps
A walk so elegant commoners and Kings alike worshipped the ground beneath her feet.
Marilyn showed me the thrills of fervent, passionate love
And its devilish perils.
She taught me how easily love fills your heart with warmth
And how quickly it turns that same knife,
Spilling your love onto the remains of your memories
Like blood on the cold concrete
Leaving nothing but a bitter carcass for the vultures to feed on.
Marilyn was my first love and my last
And I continued to love her to this very day.

Until I met you.

Her name is Sam.
Thoughtful, genuine, and stunning is she.
The way her voice sings through my ears
Like a song written just for me
The piano keys striking the walls of my heart with every breath.
She has a smile that lights up the world with one flash
So bright and beaming it blinds me
From the night terrors haunting me.
Her laugh ripples through my vertebrae,
Giving me chills as I watch her happiness in slow motion.
The mortal man was not built to understand such purity
But her euphoria is so raw and so true
To be restrained by the meek descriptions words can offer.
Her love is the medium my light travels through.
She amplifies the silence in me with her gentle empathy
Allowing me to express myself without uttering a word.
She gave me life when my soul needed saving
She gave me definition when my words lacked meaning

She gave me strength when my convictions lacked fortitude
She gave me love when my heart needed emotion.

As perceptive and thoughtful as Sage
As complex and loving as Amelie
As gorgeous and alluring as Marilyn

Sam.

Monsoon

I wish I could do more.
It's tragic how small we can be.
Our eternity is but an insignificant drop in an ocean
Our efforts to become ubiquitous are transgressions against the tide.
We can only sit idly by and hide whenever He weeps
And weep She does.
I can hear the pain that roars out thunderously from the clouds
As God's tears soak up the Earth.
He cries deafeningly for His children who are kidnapped and forced to murder-
For His beautiful forests burning to the ground
While the ash and smoke blend in with the carcinogens and smog up above-
For the families with no home, no food, and worst of all no hope-
For the cities razed to the ground by Tomahawk missiles they never saw coming-
For His disciples criminally misconstruing His words for political gain-
For those who believe that He has neglected them.
And so I look out the window and wonder how I can help
But my sparks can't ignite and my waves only ripple.
They don't want to see God cry any longer.
They're building up a shield of carbon dioxide faster than ever before
Denying His existence and supplanting themselves as stronger and more worldly than He.
The world has become unbearably dry and cold
Time is running out.
And so I weep, too.

Moon

Pull me closer into your orbit.
I wanna be by your side as you drift through infinity.
Draw me in and never let me go
Because I was a reckless nomad wandering from heartbreak to heartache for much too long
Before I felt your gravity holding me down.
I've never minded living in your shadow
As you absorb all the precious light.
Watching you shine is a sight I'd give up everything for.
Your radiance reflects warmly on my apathetic surface-
Invigorating and alluring, your luminescent spirit breathes new air into my atmosphere.
From a distance, I can see your storms and all your seasons and temperaments.
I'm not afraid of the wrath of your violent turbulence-
I adore your presence all the same.
Give me time to learn to love my barren exoskeleton
So that I can eclipse the shadows of your past and shield you from the perverting light.
Because everybody tires of the spotlight once in a while.
Shooting stars come streaking by across the void,
Bringing wonder and intrigue through my spine
But nothing compares to your iridescent magnificence
Beaming so effortlessly and flawlessly through my world.

You Should Try Them

I swear to you I'm not crazy.
I saw the long scaled dragon fly over the moon;
Its wings towered over the city skyline
Its red scales shielding the ultraviolet bullets.
I watched as it breathed an icy fire onto the floating cars down below.
My hand twitched as I tried to keep hold of my balance
While teetering over the edge of denial.
To be honest with you, I wasn't scared.
I was ecstatic.
My body went numb as I stood their motionless
A rainbow shot through the sky
Glitter rained down from the Heavens and scattered over the streets like golden snowflakes.
I grabbed a fistful of sunshine and brought it up to my nose.
Its sweet aroma of life and warmth captivated me.
I wanted more.
So I jumped.

And landed on the side of a breathtaking slope of frosty snow.
I skied down the mountain with my tongue hanging out of my mouth
Tasting every drop of serenity that passed my way.
I felt invincible.
My body jumped out of my head and began sprinting towards the finish line.
I was running through the snow like a lion chasing its prey-
My heart was pounding vehemently I was sure of it
But nothing seemed to be moving within me.
I watched myself take flight.

I was soaring over the hills and through the trees so effortlessly.
I truly felt like a superhero gliding between high rise skyscrapers.
I just needed my heroine by my side.
My partner in crime
My emotional crutch
My anchor.

Someone to drag me back down to fantasy and away from Earth.
A slow burning flame that flickers quietly into dust and silence.

She burned her lips when she put me up to her mouth.
She inhaled a breath of crackling smoke and let out a long sigh.
Her exasperation was met by a tingling sensation of guilt in her brain.
I continued to rest in her hand for a minute.
How I wanted to help her.
How I wanted her to need me.
But she grabbed the bottle and left me to dry (die) in the November rain.

Chemical Imbalance

I awoke to a torrential downpour of doubt and uncertainty:
My body trembles as the soles of my feet slam blindly on the still floor,
Ignorantly apathetic to the weight of the ghastly chains dragging painfully behind me.
Trapped in the void of my chaotic emotions, my existence stutters.
Sometimes I feel like I'm stumbling counterclockwise down the solemn path in front of me;
Guided by the shadow of the moon
My heart is forever stuck behind the darkside of my indecision.
I've found fervor and passion in the smiles of others.
Manufacturing happiness that strangers can wear on their beaming faces
But I can't take any home for myself.
They say joy is best spread around
I just think I'm immune to that airborne contagion.
Allergic to love and locked out of serotonin
I medicate in the empty recesses of my mind just to feel a semblance of emotion.
The faster I run, the longer the road gets
Until I collapse under the weight of my demons.
Blood spills from my mouth as I succumb to the claws gashing at my soul.
Euphoria kisses my lips gently as I stare into her vacant eyes.
The scythe swings over her head as death and my inhibitions collide.

Family

Dear Sara,

I'm sorry I wasn't around to protect you.
My heart wanted to turn around and come back
But the money hijacked my life and pressed a gun to my head
Telling me to take a different route
Over turnpikes and unpaved roads
Into the cracked and crooked streets that never see the light of day.
They call it a ghost town-
Not because the streets are empty but because the demons, they follow and haunt you:
The bodies you've watched fall right in front of you-
Guns, knives, drugs
It's a tragedy but by now it's just Thursday to you.
I wanted to be a good father to you but I was too busy trying to make up for lost time-
A lost cause consumed with revenge and spite
Blinded by an unrelenting anger that pulsates through every blood vessel-
Filled with resentment for a childhood robbed-
Empty because of a childhood robbed.
I watched my brother disappear into thin air,
Watched my mother lose her battle with a shameless, merciless God,
Watched my father catch a bullet with his name engraved on the side fired from the handgun clasped between my two adolescent, shaking hands.
But I didn't watch J leave.
I didn't watch my mother during her last precious breaths of life while fading into oblivion on her death bed.
I was a coward who couldn't face the tides he created when he desecrated his own world.
I murdered my own father out of fear.
Couldn't even look him in the eyes while he was fighting back defending all our lives.
I thought I could fix our family
I guess I messed up.

J joined a gang and lit up the block, killing every last one of the bangers he thought took his father's life.
J then took over Mac's business and got murdered two years later.
I killed my brother and now I know why
I stay up at night crying silently while the agonizing screams from my mother's spirit echo through my house.
I killed my mother and now I know why
I won't allow myself to get close to my only daughter.
I understand now that I'm a cursed child of His.
Death trails in my every footstep and collects victims in its macabre wake.
I spent three years hunting down and murdering and robbing every member of J's enemies until there weren't enough bodies left to fill the chamber in the .45.
The only person I can't seem to kill is myself
And Lord knows I've tried.
My hope is that you'll learn to grow up to be a beautiful, independent woman
But I'm sorry in advance for not being there to bear witness to your proudest moments
Because I love you and it breaks my heart to not be our father.
But I'm the grim reaper with a bad case of muscle atrophy
And I refuse to hold another body of a loved one in my callous arms.

With all my love,
    Your father,

        Dre

Incandescent

I remember when I saw you shine for the first time.
My eyes rushed to convince my mind that it was real
Before the image could fade away just far enough from my memories
The way you stood by the fire
Motionless
At ease
Your smile resting gently on your face
Brought such invigorating warmth to my frigid countenance.
The smoke always seemed to clear so that the stars could see their most divine reflection.
I've always wondered who was lucky enough to have been able to capture and hold on to your light
Because my vested share merely flickers in the dull absence of my heart.

That was a long time ago.

My frostbitten fingers have not felt kindness in years
And my eyes scan blankly as the world passes me by.
The current that powers my spirit has shut off
And I desperately cling to glimpses of love that flash through my body
Just to watch it fade into bitter darkness.
As you faded.

Me

I don't want to waste your time so let's just get into it
Let me remind you that I'm the greatest to ever do this shit
I'm not just a visionary:
You dream it, I do it.
The doors they slammed in my face now I crash right through them.
I was born from excellence.
I let them spit on my name
And watched as they robbed me of my pride-
Beat me blue until no more blood poured out onto the concrete.
They sewed my mouth shut but couldn't steal my voice.
I wake up every morning empowered and optimistic
That my words will sneak off the page and touch the most guarded hearts.
I always had a dream to change the world somehow-
To impact it in this lifetime.
My biggest fear was not being able to do enough
But I see with paramount clarity what I am now.
I'm a motherfucking champion.
I walk the Earth with supreme confidence boasting from every quaking step.
The doubts escaping their prison in my mind rattle their chains in contempt
As my cationic synapses eviscerate them from the forefront of my attention.

I used to question my worthiness to breathe the same air as the living
I used to wonder if I would be able to make something out of nothing
I used to scream into the suffocating emptiness of my emotions just to fall asleep
I used to swallow my inhibitions to put on a smile
I used to want to kill myself to escape the pain of living.

I can see beyond the ethereal horizon now;
As the sun peeks over the hills
My heart beats to a different rhythm.

Now I hear the silent conversations.
Now they like to sing my praises.
Now they cheer my name.
Now my blood flows warmly and evenly.
Now they want to be me.
Now they recite my poems.
Now they understand.
Now they know. Now they too can see.
That I'm ready to take my place on my throne.
King of the fractured and champion of my truth.
Now they crave and yearn to hear my next word.
Nobody gave a damn to listen to me
But now they all want a glimpse into my thoughts.
So let me welcome you to my contagious mind…

Legacy

Go forth and be great, my child.
For it is the pursuit of happiness that keeps us alive.
Stretch your hands and reach out farther than they'll ever let you
And grab hold of all you wish to obtain.
You can always see beyond what first appears
Be relentless and seize that which is owed to you
Because the wolves they threw you to won't look out for you.
Ambition is driven and success is inspired.
Greatness is taken by those who can handle its strength;
So I ask you:
Will you be enough?

It is not sufficient to stamp your mark on this world
But you must shatter the chains which constrain your insecurities
Be open to vulnerability and do not fear shame.
Love yourself and be proud of the imperfection facing you in the mirror.

Most of all, continue to learn.
Learning breeds innovation and stalls complacency.
Do not allow yourself to sit idly as the market transforms without you.

Please don't forget me.
For all I have to leave behind are words on a page
Words that can crumble when mistreated
Words that can fade if neglected
Words that can linger if left unconfronted.
Please forgive me
But please don't forget me.

Release

Sentenced to death by my own wisdom
My thoughts lining me up for execution
The brightest star in my mind
Would not escape the darkest corners of the universe
Time stands still on death row
It rests eternally for the damned and the broken
They ask me what my preference is
The only decision left I have control over
The chair would only incite my body back to life
A needle would only bring my blood back into circulation
So I asked them to put the heat to my head
And blow my fucking brains out
Murder thy enemy and murder thyself
Put to sleep the devilish thoughts intoxicating my brain
I died when I lost my convictions
To the pressure of being sane
As I lay on my death bed
The warmth in my heart sends shivers down my neck
As the life inside of me withers
I can see the darkness consuming my soul
As I step forward into the bright atrium
I close my eyes, turning the chapter in my mind
I feel the cold metal of the revolver barrel on my temple
I look up at the strange man in front of me
And ask him to let me pull the trigger
My breathing slows but remains light
I've never been more calm.
My finger twitches and the last I hear is the clicking of metal before a brief glimpse of heat sears into my head the bullet already homicidal my body collapses time's up time's up it's over.
It's over.

Made in the USA
Las Vegas, NV
31 March 2025